MW00901287

DILLY DUCK
PLANS A PARADE

BY **Holly DiBella-McCarthy**
ILLUSTRATED BY **Pradyut Chatterjee**

Dilly Duck Plans a Parade

All rights reserved. Published by Book Chatter Press.
Book Chatter Press, P.O. Box 1474, Little River, SC 29566
bookchatterpress.com
hollydibellamccarthy.com

ISBN: Hardcover 979-8-9883308-2-0
ISBN: Paperback 979-8-9883308-3-7

Library of Congress Control Number: 2023912844

To Brendan Patrick McCarthy

Thank you for being the inspiration for my Billy Beaver character.
Your strong work ethic, thirst for new knowledge,
and compassionate heart make you a *grand marshal*
in the parade of life.

HDM

Tap, tap, tap . . .

Dilly Duck tap-tapped her beak upon the lodge's door.
She tapped so hard the shelter shook from
its roof right down to its floor.

"Wake up Billy Beaver.
I'm here to ask for help today.
We want to make a
colorful parade.
Can you help us?
What do you say?"

Billy yawned and stretched
in his den on a bank in Wonder Wake.
Why must he rise after working all night
on his dam in the lake?

Tap, tap, tap . . .

The tapping got louder and louder,
and it seemed that it just wouldn't end,
so Billy Beaver swam under the water and
surfaced to welcome his friend.

Dilly Duck splashed in the lake and
greeted her pal with a shout,
excited to share what the crew's fun
and fancy plan was all about.

"Today is parade day!
So far, we have ten little
ducks for the line.

Let's gather colors
around the lake
so our ducky parade
will shine!"

"I can chop," sighed Billy, "and build woody places.
I'm strong and I'm wonderfully fit.
But finding colors that cannot be seen,
I'd not be much help, not one tiny bit."

Dilly's friend was color-blind,
so he didn't see that well,
but Billy still could help because
his other skills were swell.

"Seeing brown is easy for you,
but there are many colors to be found.
Let's work together to find those colors
by smell, by touch, and by sound."

So off paddled Billy
with his nose in the air,

sniff,

sniff,

sniff.

Back in a flash,
loud chatter was heard.
"I only found brown,
but take a whiff!"

Delighted, Dilly laughed and flapped
and let out a quack and a coo.
Billy's nose had really discovered
some pink, some purple, and blue.

Then Dilly gathered some green
to build a flat, unsinkable boat,
to make sure all the sweet-smelling
colors would safely stay afloat.

Billy Beaver swam away a pleased and
happy fellow,

and came back
with lovely shades of
orange, black, and yellow.

All the colors that Billy had found
were felt with his paws and his face.

"Wow!" Dilly beamed.
"There are so many colors
hiding all over this place!"

As Dilly worked,
Billy's ears were wiggling up and down.

Then Billy Beaver
returned with
red, and white and . . .

brown!

"You found some brown," whistled Dilly,
"by the croak of a frog that you heard,
and white from a swan's flapping wings,
and red from a chirping bird."

"Look here on the float;
even though your sight is poor, you smelled blue.
And these other colors you sensed by touch
and by sound - how clever are you!"

"Thank you, friend," proud Billy gushed,
"for showing me that I can see well enough."

The flock then saw their friends returning,
towing some colorful stuff.

With honks and hoots and quacks galore,
the ducks sang a favorite chime.

"Friends help friends!

Let's go! Lineup! It's parade time!"

QUESTIONS FOR READERS AND SUPER LISTENERS:

- How would you feel if you couldn't see very well?

- What would you like to do if you went to Wonder Wake?

- Why is Dilly Duck a good friend?

- How many rhyming words can you find in this story?

- What new words did you hear in this story?

- Where can you find color to make your own parade?

Find free resources for kids and a free

S.T.R.E.T.CH before, during & after reading
Activity-Resource Guide at:

www.hollydibellamccarthy.com

If you were a beaver, you would . . .

- ◆ love your waterproof fur, webbed feet, paws with fingers, and scaly flat tail.

- ◆ have very poor eyesight and may also have color-blindness.

- ◆ hear sounds from far away both on land and underwater.

- ◆ sniff to find food to eat, such as leaves, roots, twigs, and aquatic plants.

- ◆ topple trees with your two-inch long orange teeth to use for dam building and teeth trimming.

- ◆ live in a dome-shaped lodge with underwater tunnels.

- ◆ hold your breath for up to 15 minutes underwater, and swim as fast as a speedboat going 35 miles per hour.

ABOUT THE AUTHOR

Like Dilly Duck, **Holly DiBella-McCarthy** likes to keep very busy. She loves reading, writing, and brainstorming new ideas with others. Learning facts about animals is fun for Holly. She has had her own cats, dogs, bunnies, birds, fish, and yes, even a duck named Dilly! Holly loves family time and often travels to New England from her home in North Carolina to visit. She also enjoys exploring new places and traveling to new beach towns in the United States and beyond. Holly has taught students in preschool through college. Her picture books are written to make learning fun for children and the adults who read to them.

ABOUT THE ILLUSTRATOR

Pradyut Chatterjee is the artist and team coordinator who created Dilly Duck and her duck friends. Pradyut understands author requirements and how story and illustration work together to foster children's positive mental health.

Pratyush Chaterjee is the illustrator who created Billy Beaver for this book. Both illustrators have spent over 15 years working in the art and entertainment business in design, publication, and digital media projects. They can be contacted at: illustrator.pub@gmail.com

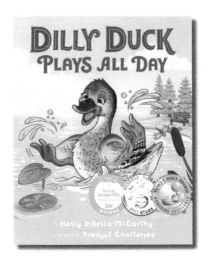

5 Star Reviews:

". . . totally encaptivating storyboard of happiness. Hopefully, Holly DiBella-McCarthy will create other adventures of this fanciful duck." Beth Adams, Pacific Book Reviewer

". . . a delightful little book that is easy to read, fun to follow, and elicited more than a few laughs - and one gasp - from my youngest reader. Holly DiBella-McCarthy is a talented kid-lit author with prose that sings off the page." Jamie Michele, Reader's Favorite Reviewer

"Kid approved, well written, great pics, my kid loved it, so there you go!" Dr. R. Ahmed, parent

"A day of counting, rhyming, and friendship is found in this happy book for young children. I recommend this well-written and well-illustrated book for both school and public libraries." Suzan B., Librarian

ON THE BANK of a great big lake in a park called Wonder Wake, Dilly Duck sits all alone, so sad and bored on her own. There is just one thing to do. Find her friends, her flock, her crew! This fun rhyming picture book will have children ages 2-6 counting to 10 as Dilly gathers her friends for a day of play.

More amazing stories and resources at:

www.hollydibellamccarthy.com

Printed in the USA
CPSIA information can be obtained
at www.ICGtesting.com
LVHW070719261023
761974LV00013B/189

9 798988 330820